S0-BBX-334

Wake up, Bear

Lynley Dodd

Gareth Stevens Children's Books

It was time for Bear to wake up.
He had been asleep for many months,
ALL winter, in fact.
Now it was Spring.

His friends came to his cave
under the Bulbul tree and said,
"Hi Bear, time to get up."
But he wouldn't wake up.
He just lay there,
smiling dozily,
and went right on
snoring.

Lion shook his mane and roared.
It was a rumbling, grumbling,
SCARY roar,
and it made everyone jump with fright.
But Bear went right on
snoring.

Squirrel dropped an acorn on Bear's nose.
BONK went the acorn,
but it didn't bother Bear.
He just went right on
snoring.

Monkey curled the end
of his long spidery tail
and tickled Bear's toes.
Bear twitched a little,
here and there,
but he still went right on
snoring.

Parrot brought her family,
uncles, grandmothers, and all.
They sat in the Bulbul tree
and squawked and screeched
until their throats were sore
and their beaks were stiff.
The noise was awful,
but Bear went right on
snoring.

Cat arched his back,
bristled his fur
and yowled,
"w . . . w . . . rr . . . OWWWWW!"
His mother could hear him a mile away,
but Bear didn't hear him at all.
He just went right on
snoring.

Elephant went down to the river
and filled her trunk with water.
She whooshed it at Bear.
SPLAT!
Bear was soaking wet,
and drips dropped off the end of his nose,
but he still went right on
snoring.

Owl sat on a twig above Bear's cave.
He took a deep breath,
until all his feathers stuck out,
and hooted,
"oo . . . ooOOOOoo."
The smallest animals hid in the grass,
but Bear went right on
snoring.

Hippo opened her mouth
and gave an enormous yawn.
It showed every one of her teeth
and her tonsils too.
She looked TERRIBLE,
but Bear didn't see her.
He just went right on
snoring.

Goat stuck up his tail,
bent down his head,
and butted Bear.
BOOMPH!
He got Bear's fur in his nose and ears,
but Bear didn't feel a thing.
He just went right on
snoring.

Snake twined and slithered
round and down the Bulbul tree.
She hissed,
"sssssssSSSSSSsssssss."
It made the animals shiver,
but not Bear.
He just kept right on
snoring.

"It's no good," said everyone sadly,
"We've roared,
bonked,
tickled,
screeched,
yowled,
whooshed,
hooted,
yawned,
butted,
and hissed ourselves silly,
and Bear WON'T wake up.
We might as well go home."

Just then a bee came buzzing past.

went the bee around Bear's head.

"HONEY!" said Bear,
and he woke up.

For a free color catalog describing Gareth Stevens' list of high-quality books, call 1-800-542-2595 (USA) or 1-800-461-9120 (Canada). Gareth Stevens' Fax: (414) 225-0377.

GOLD STAR FIRST READERS

HELP! by Nigel Croser
Picnic Pandemonium by M. Christine Butler

and by Lynley Dodd . . .

A Dragon in a Wagon
The Apple Tree
Find Me a Tiger
Hairy Maclary from Donaldson's Dairy
Hairy Maclary's Bone
Hairy Maclary Scattercat
Hairy Maclary's Caterwaul Caper
Hairy Maclary's Rumpus at the Vet

Hairy Maclary's Show Business
The Minister's Cat ABC
Schnitzel von Krumm's Basketwork
Slinky Malinki
Slinky Malinki, Open the Door
The Smallest Turtle
Wake Up, Bear

Library of Congress Cataloging-in-Publication Data

Dodd, Lynley.
    Wake up, bear.

    (Gold star first readers)
    Summary: Despite all their efforts none of the animals can get bear to wake up from his winter sleep.
    [1. Bears — Fiction. 2. Animals — Fiction] I. Title. II. Series.
PZ7.D6627Wak 1987   [E]   86-42798
ISBN 1-55532-124-0 (lib. bdg.)
ISBN 0-8368-1177-1 (trade)

North American edition first published in 1988 by

Gareth Stevens Publishing
1555 North RiverCenter Drive, Suite 201
Milwaukee, Wisconsin 53212, USA

First published in New Zealand by Mallinson Rendel Publishers Ltd.
Copyright © 1986 by Lynley Dodd.

All rights reserved. No part of this book may be reproduced or used in any form or by any means without permission in writing from Gareth Stevens, Inc.

Printed in MEXICO

5 6 7 8 9 10 11 12 99 98 97 96 95 94